DERRYDALE BOOKS
New York

This 1984 edition is published by Derrydale Books,
distributed by Crown Publishers Inc.
© Peter Haddock Ltd, Bridlington, U.K.
Printed in Hungary

ISBN 0-517-43878-X
HGFEDCBA

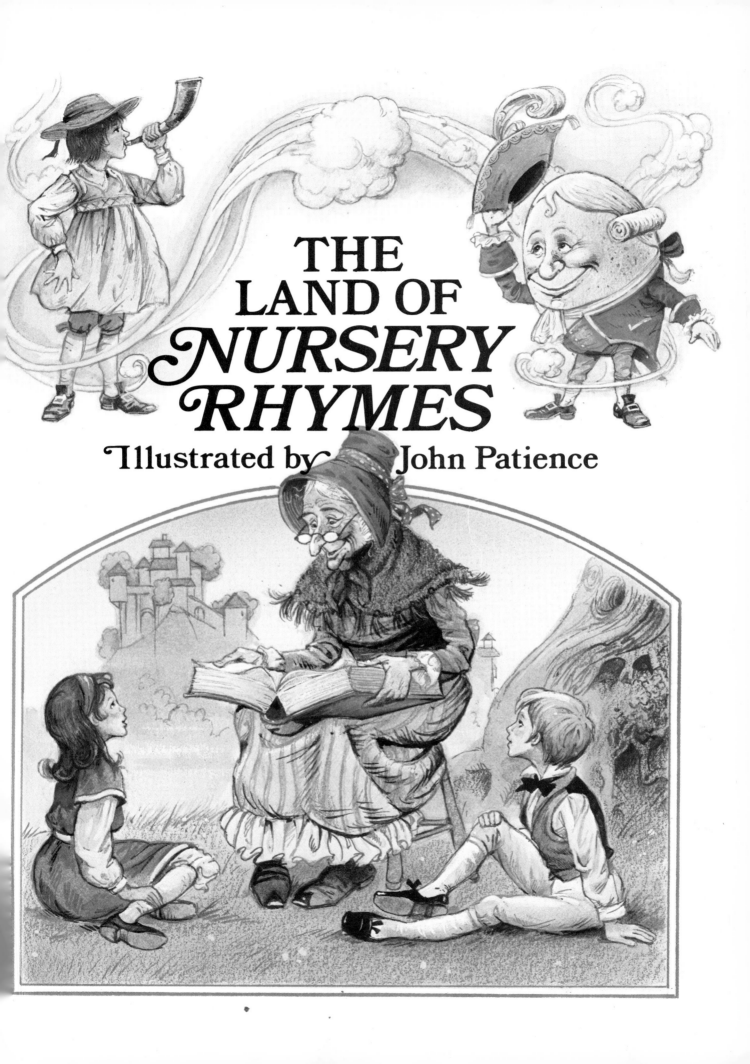

THE LAND OF NURSERY RHYMES

Illustrated by John Patience

Humpty Dumpty sat on a wall,
Humpty Dumpty had a great fall,
All the king's horses,
And all the king's men,
Couldn't put Humpty together again.

Tom, Tom, the piper's son,
Stole a pig and away he run;
The pig was eat and Tom was beat,
And Tom went howling
  down the street.

Rub-a-dub-dub
Three men in a tub,
And who do you think they be?
The butcher, the baker,
The candlestick-maker,
And they all sailed out to sea.

Three blind mice, see how they run!
They all ran after the farmer's wife,
Who cut off their tails with a carving knife,
Did you ever see such a thing in your life,
As three blind mice.

Jack and Jill went up the hill
To fetch a pail of water;
Jack fell down and broke his crown,
And Jill came tumbling after.

Up Jack got, and home did trot,
As fast as he could caper,
He went to bed, to mend his head
With vinegar and brown paper.

One misty, moisty morning,
When cloudy was the weather,
I chanced to meet an old man
Clothed all in leather.
He began to compliment,
and I began to grin.
How do you do?
And how do you do?
And how do you do again?

Mary, Mary, quite contrary, how does
your garden grow?
With silver bells and cockle shells, and
pretty maids all in a row.

Jack be nimble, Jack be
quick,
And Jack jump over
the candle-stick.

Ladybird, ladybird
Fly away home,
Your house is on fire
And your children all gone;
All except one
And that's little Ann
And she has crept under
The frying-pan

Jack Sprat could eat no fat, his wife could eat no lean,
And so between them both, you see, they licked the platter clean.

If all the seas were one sea,
What a GREAT sea that would be!
If all the trees were one tree,
What a GREAT tree that would be!
And if all the axes were one axe,
What a GREAT axe that would be!
And if all the men were one man,
What a GREAT man that would be!
And if the GREAT man took the
    GREAT axe,
And cut down the GREAT tree,
And let it fall into the GREAT sea,
What a splish-splash that would be!

Baa, baa, black sheep,
Have you any wool?
Yes sir, yes sir,
Three bags full;
One for the master,
And one for the dame,
And one for the little boy
Who lives down the lane.

See-saw, Margery Daw,
Jacky shall have a new master;
Jacky shall have but a penny a day,
Because he can't work any faster.

Little Miss Muffet
Sat on a tuffet,
Eating her curds and whey;
There came a big spider,
Who sat down beside her
And frightened Miss Muffet
away.

If all the world were paper,
And all the seas were ink,
If all the trees were bread
    and cheese,
What should we have to drink.

There was an old woman
Who lived in a shoe,
She had so many children
She didn't know what to do;
She gave them some broth
Without any bread,
She whipped them all soundly
And put them to bed.

There was an old woman tossed up in a basket,
Seventy times as high as the moon;
Where she was going I couldn't but ask her,
For in her hand, she carried a broom.
"Old woman, old woman, old woman," quoth I,
"Whither, O whither, O whither so high?"
"To sweep the cobwebs off the sky!"
"May I go with you?"
"Aye, by and by."

Hey diddle diddle,
The cat and the fiddle,
The cow jumped over the moon;
The little dog laughed
To see such sport,
And the dish ran away with the spoon.

Twinkle, twinkle, little star,
How I wonder what you are.
Up above the world so high,
Like a diamond in the sky. -

When the blazing sun is gone,
When he nothing shines upon,
Then you show your little light,
Twinkle, twinkle, all the night.

Then the traveler in the dark,
Thanks you for your tiny spark,
He could not see which way to go,
If you did not twinkle so.

Little Boy Blue, come blow up
　　　your horn!
The sheep's in the meadow, the
　　　cow's in the corn!
Where is the boy who looks
　　　after the sheep?
He's under the haystack, fast
　　　asleep!

Will you wake him? No not I,
For if I do, he's sure to cry.

Hickory, dickory, dock,
The mouse ran up the clock.
The clock struck one,
The mouse ran down,
Hickory, dickory, dock.

Goosey, goosey gander,
Whither shall I wander?
Upstairs and downstairs
And in my lady's chamber.
There I met an old man
Who would not say his
     prayers.
I took him by the left leg
And threw him down the
     stairs.

Old King Cole
Was a merry old soul,
And a merry old soul was he;
He called for his pipe,
And he called for his bowl,
And he called for his fiddlers three.

Every fiddler, he had a fiddle,
And a very fine fiddle had he;
Twee tweedle dee, tweedle dee, went the fiddlers.
Oh, there's none so rare
As can compare
With King Cole and his fiddlers three.

Doctor Foster went to
  Gloucester
In a shower of rain:
He stepped in a puddle

Right up to his
  middle,
And never went
  there again.

Wee Willie Winkie
Runs through the town,
Upstairs and downstairs,
In his nightgown.

Calling through the window,
Crying through the lock,
"Are all the children in their
        beds?"
"It's past eight o'clock!"

The lion and the unicorn
Were fighting for the crown;
The lion beat the unicorn
All around the town.

Some gave them white bread,
And some gave them brown;
Some gave them plum cake
And drummed them out of town.

Ding dong bell,
Pussy's in the well.
Who put her in?
Little Johnny Green.
Who pulled her out?
Little Tommy Stout.

What a naughty boy was that
To try and drown poor pussy cat,
Who never did any harm,
But killed all the mice
In his father's barn.

Old Mother Goose,
When she wanted to wander,
Would ride through the air
On a very fine gander.

To market, to market, to buy
    a fat pig,
Home again, home again, jiggety jig.

To market, to market, to buy a fat hog,
Home again, home again,
    joggety jog.

Little Tommy Tittlemouse
Lived in a little house;
He caught fishes
In other men's ditches.

The man in the moon,
Came down too soon,
And asked the way to Norwich.
He went by the south,
And burned his mouth,
While eating cold plum porridge!

I saw a ship a-sailing,
A-sailing on the sea,
And it was fully laden
With pretty things for me.

There were sweeties in the cabin,
And apples in the hold.
The sails were made of silk
And the masts were made of gold.

The four and twenty sailors,
That ran along the decks,
Were four and twenty white mice
With chains about their necks.

The Captain was a duck,
With stripes all down his back,
And when the ship began to move,
The Captain said, "Quack, quack!"

There was a crooked man
And he walked a crooked mile,
And he found a crooked sixpence,
Beside a crooked stile

He bought a crooked cat,
Which caught a crooked mouse,
And they all lived together
In a crooked little house.

Hush-a-bye, baby, on the tree top,
When the wind blows the cradle
 will rock;
When the bough breaks the cradle
 will fall,
Down will come baby, cradle and all.

Sing a song of sixpence,
A pocket full of rye;
Four and twenty blackbirds,
Baked in a pie.

When the pie was opened,
The birds began to sing;
Was not that a dainty dish,
To set before the king?